2/21

YOU
are awesome!

Susann Hoffmann

PHILOMEL BOOKS

You can be . . .

You can be...

FUNNY

You can be...

SMART

You can be...

FAST

You can be...

CALM

You can be...

BOLD

You can be...

You can be . . .

CLEVER

You can be . . .

SILLY

You can be...

You can be...

LOVING

You can be...

BRAVE

You can be...
CREATIVE

You can be...

HELPFUL

You can be anything.

You are awesome.

PHILOMEL BOOKS
An imprint of Penguin Random House LLC, New York

First published in the United States of America by Philomel,
an imprint of Penguin Random House LLC, 2020.

Visit us online at penguinrandomhouse.com

Library of Congress Cataloging-in-Publication Data is available.

Manufactured in China.

ISBN 9780593202180

1 3 5 7 9 10 8 6 4 2

Edited by Liza Kaplan. Design by Lori Thorn.
Text set in Metallophile Sp8.